FLYING FURBALLS

Kit-napped

DONOVAN BIXLEY

upstart press

In memory of Jelly, one of the good guys.

Remember to feed your pets appropriate food.
The characters in this book are only *pretending*
to eat raspberry cream puffs.

A catalogue record for this book is available from the
National Library of New Zealand

ISBN 978-1-988516-16-5

An Upstart Press Book
Published in 2018 by Upstart Press Ltd
Level 4, 15 Huron St, Takapuna
Auckland, New Zealand

Printed by 1010 Printing International Limited, China

MEET SOME OF THE CHARACTERS AT CATs HQ

Claude D'Bonair is a fearless young pilot in the CATs Air Corps. He's always ready to throw himself into dangerous situations — but sometimes he throws himself in *before* thinking. Claude loves to try new things and experience different cultures.

Syd Fishus flew the first aeroplanes with Claude's father before the war. Syd is often thinking about his belly, like how to keep it in shape — a round shape! He has a fondness for dessert, but he hates the desert.

C-for is CATs' secret weapon, forever inventing crazy new gadgets. He has dog and cat friends who share his love of music and science.

Best friends **Sinja** and **Mitzi** are dedicated nurses in the CATs Medical Corps. Sinja is a qualified ambulance driver, and Mitzi is training to be a doctor.

Manx is never happier than when she has a wrench in her hand and something to fix. Being CATs' head mechanic is a busy job, but Manx also has to keep an eye out for her two kit sisters: fidgeting **Wigglebum**, and ever-curious **Picklepurr**.

Commander Katerina Snookums is the head of CATs Air Corps. **General Fluffington** is her right-hand man, along with his secretary, **Mr Tiddles**.

Major Ginger Tom thinks he's the cat's pyjamas, and so does everyone else.

Mrs Cushion lives to serve in the armed forces — but usually she's just serving her prize-winning cream puffs.

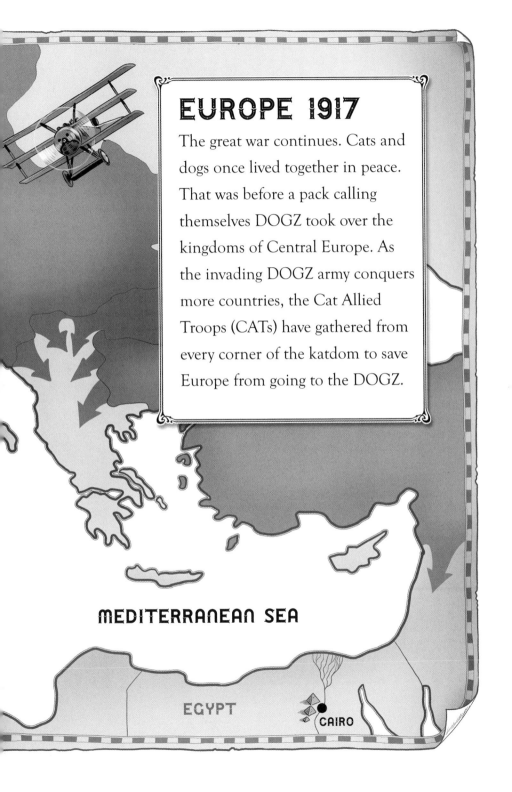

EUROPE 1917

The great war continues. Cats and dogs once lived together in peace. That was before a pack calling themselves DOGZ took over the kingdoms of Central Europe. As the invading DOGZ army conquers more countries, the Cat Allied Troops (CATs) have gathered from every corner of the katdom to save Europe from going to the DOGZ.

MEDITERRANEAN SEA

EGYPT

CAIRO

CHATEAU FUR-DE-LYS

CATs headquarters (HQ) on the outskirts of Paris. Claude's fighter squadron is based here, and it's also Command Centre for all secret missions.

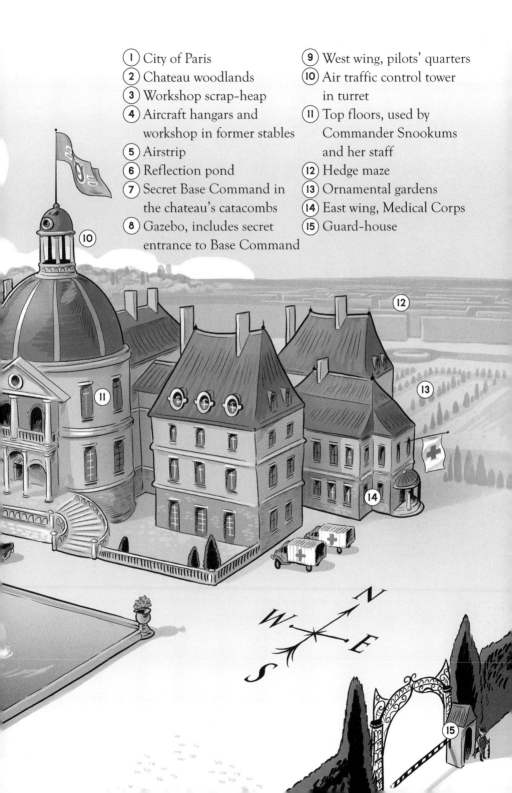

1. City of Paris
2. Chateau woodlands
3. Workshop scrap-heap
4. Aircraft hangars and workshop in former stables
5. Airstrip
6. Reflection pond
7. Secret Base Command in the chateau's catacombs
8. Gazebo, includes secret entrance to Base Command
9. West wing, pilots' quarters
10. Air traffic control tower in turret
11. Top floors, used by Commander Snookums and her staff
12. Hedge maze
13. Ornamental gardens
14. East wing, Medical Corps
15. Guard-house

DOGE

THE MIDDAY
SUN

CHAPTER 1

'**M**iserable moggies!' screeched Alf Alpha. 'They call me "sausage dog"! I'm not, I'm not, I'm NOT! I'm a *pure-bred dachshund*.' The Dear Leader of the Dog Obedience Governed Zone, or DOGZ as they called themselves, was propped up in bed in his luxurious mountain hideaway, The Hound's Tooth.

Since declaring war on all cats, Alf Alpha was obsessed with reading the latest cat newspapers from around the world to find out what they said about him. Today he was getting angrier by the second.

'They call The Hound's Tooth a "Poopy Puppy Pit",' he snarled, turning red.

'They say I am a "whining wiener",' he frothed, his tiny sausage-dog body leaping out from under the sheets.

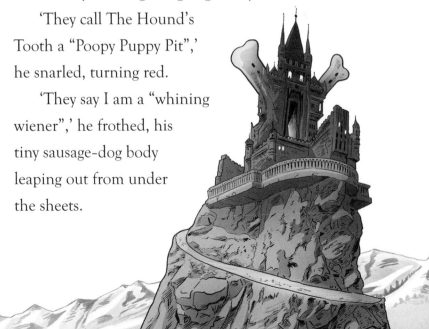

Alf Alpha slammed down the newspaper. 'How *dare* those cats make fun of my stature. Very soon they will find I am *not* so short when it comes to ideas. Once our secret weapon is completed, cats everywhere will cower before the DOGZ new world order.'

Alf Alpha's top commander, General Dogsbody, stood impatiently at the foot of the bed. 'My Furrer,' he said. 'What *are* today's orders?'

The Furrer wriggled and squiggled himself back under the covers, turning around several times before he was comfortable. 'My first order for today is spare ribs and BBQ sauce, with a side bone to chew.'

'No, My Furrer,' sighed General Dogsbody. 'Today's *battle* orders.'

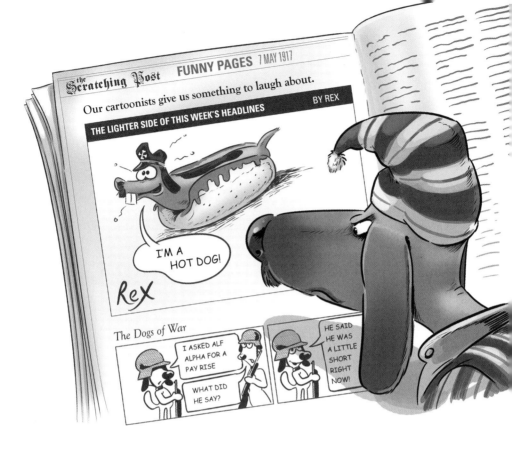

Alf Alpha snatched up the newspaper and pointed to a cartoon.

'I want you to find this Rex, whoever he is,' screeched The Furrer. 'I want a whole battalion sent to rub his nose in it. We'll cut this scribbling scoundrel down to size.'

'That's a *tall* order . . .' began General Dogsbody.

'What did you say?' said Alf Alpha.

'I mean, we're *short* on soldiers . . .' continued the General.

'How dare you!'

'It's a *little* . . .'

'Enough!' snapped The Furrer. 'I won't be mocked!'

General Dogsbody rolled his eyes. The Cat Allied Troops had halted the DOGZ army by flooding the main route to the front lines. Two of the DOGZ top commanders, Sergeant Wolfgang and The Red Setter, were injured during the attack. General Dogsbody wished The Furrer would spend more time on battle orders than sulking over cartoons or coming up with crazy ideas, like secret weapons and kit-napping cat scientists.

'Only a dog like *me* can rule the world,' The Furrer was saying. 'I will march into Paris and every cat will look up to me. *Then* we'll see who's a wiener!'

The only way cats would look up to Alf Alpha would be if he was standing on a ladder, General Dogsbody thought to himself. Of course the General didn't say this. Mentioning his height was one of The Furrer's pet hates.

The Furrer was in full ranting mode now. 'We'll see how clever those cats are without their top inventor. "Project Sphinx" is almost completed, and when it is ...' – The Furrer cackled an evil laugh – 'CATs will be *fleaing* for their lives. *Bwha ha ha ha ha.*'

He turned to General Dogsbody. 'It's time to begin phase one. Order the flyers to be sent out.'

Far from Alf Alpha's mountaintop lair, another gathering was taking place. At CATs HQ on the outskirts of Paris the entire CATs squadron was also in bed, however *they* were *not* wearing their pyjamas. They were wrapped from their whiskers to their paws in bandages, in the hospital wing.

'This is simply a *catastrophe*!' wailed Nurse Sinja. 'How on earth did this happen?'

'I've been asking myself the same thing,' moaned Claude D'Bonair. The young pilot was bound up in a hospital bed. 'I shouldn't be here,' Claude grumbled. 'Syd, I blame you — and your stomach — for getting us into this mess.'

Claude's old friend Syd Fishus was in the next bed over. Syd had been like a father to Claude, but right now he looked more like a mummy.

Nurse Sinja walked up and down the rows of bandaged pilots, before turning to the group of nurses following behind her. 'These bandages have been done completely wrong. You're going to have to start all over again.'

Nurse Sinja was running a medical training course and had asked the pilots to pretend to be patients for her nursing students, with one promise. 'Mate, I only volunteered because Sinja said we'd get raspberry cream puffs,' said Syd.

'I've had enough of this,' said Claude. 'We've got important missions to fly.'

'I dunno, mate,' said Syd. 'I can think of worse things than lying in bed all day. But until I've had those promised cream puffs, I'm not doing any more.'

'Doing any *more?*' scoffed Claude. 'All you've done is lie about all day.'

'Too right!' grinned Syd. 'I've been working *flat out.*'

At that moment, Mrs Cushion rolled into the hospital wing with her tea trolley, which looked like it was about to topple over with bright red raspberry cream puffs dripping with sticky sweet jam. Syd sprang up in bed. Claude could almost see Syd's eyes drooling. *Finally*, thought Claude, *something to get Syd out of bed.*

'Tut tut tut, Sydney,' scolded Nurse Sinja.
'Mrs Cushion's pudding trolley will have to wait
until we've redone *all* these bandages.'

Syd's terrible wail filled the air as he watched
Mrs Cushion's tea trolley trundle away.

'And . . .' smiled Nurse Sinja. 'Mitzi needs to demonstrate proper injection technique.'

Nurse Mitzi was training to be a doctor. She picked up a syringe and tested the plunger. A drop of medicine squirted out of the needle tip.

Another terrible wail filled the air. It took a while for Claude to realise that this time it *wasn't* Syd.

It was air raid sirens!

'DOGZ bombers!' cried Claude.

Everyone froze. Eyes scanned the roof, as if they would be able to see straight through it. The CATs' most famous dogfighter, Major Ginger Tom, leapt out of his bed. It *is* possible that Major Tom was intending to race for his fighter plane, however, we'll never know, because he backed into Mitzi who was carrying the large needle. He gave a surprised yelp as the needle plunged into his backside. His eyes spun upwards like a roller blind, then he fell unconscious, flat on his face.

Someone screamed.

Then chaos gripped the room — beds were overturned as cats dived underneath them. Mrs Cushion's tea trolley was sent spinning. Raspberry cream puffs sailed through the air. Pilots tore at their bandages. Some of the cats dashed for the bomb shelter in the basement.

Claude wasn't about to let those DOGZ bombers flatten Paris. He raced to the door, and out onto the airfield.

In the hospital wing cats were squeezed under furniture, waiting for the whistle of falling bombs. Raspberry cream puffs splattered the walls like a horror scene. After a few moments, Claude wandered back inside. 'You can all come out now,' Claude said casually. 'It's not what you think.'

Meanwhile, in his second-storey office, General Fluffington heard the air raid siren and looked out over CATs HQ. What he saw gave him the most tremendous shock. He pulled his whiskers to make sure he wasn't dreaming – but he was awake alright! By the time he had raced downstairs, the scene was like something from one of his worst nightmares.

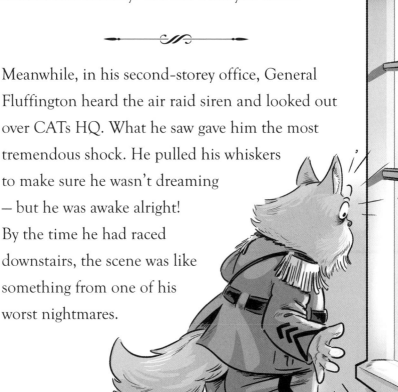

Pilots from the CATs fighter squadron were lurching about the airfield like an army of the dead. Gory red stains splattered their bandaged bodies. Vacant eyes turned skyward.

General Fluffington came across the bulging form of Captain Syd Fishus, looking like the cat who'd got the cream, with Claude by his side.

'What the blazes is this?!' spluttered General
Fluffington.

'Raspberry cream puffs,' said Syd, dipping his
finger into a splodge on his belly.

'Sydney, you wobble-headed wombat,' bellowed
the General. 'Not that. *This* . . .' he pointed skyward.
High above, the DOGZ bombers droned on. Behind
them trailed a flittering of white flecks. It looked as
if the bombers were dropping snow.

At that moment, Major Tom was carried past on a stretcher. Nurse Sinja was fussing along behind. 'The hospital's an absolute wreck,' Sinja was saying. 'We have to move Major Tom back to his own quarters.'

'I'm *flying*,' burbled Major Tom. The injection had made him as giddy as a goldfish.

'That's a scene you won't find in Major Tom's autobiography,' said Claude.

'No,' laughed Syd. 'He doesn't like to be the butt of any jokes.'

'This is no joke,' growled General Fluffington. 'With Major Tom out of action, you two are now my top officers.'

Syd drew himself up and tried to look dignified, which was difficult because he was wrapped in bandages and splattered with cream puffs. 'You have my full-cream attention, I mean . . . I'll be pudding serious thought, I mean . . . I'll put my full weight behind it, sir.'

By now the white specks had drifted lower. They were pieces of paper. Claude snatched one out of the air as they started touching down across the airfield.

'Those bombers are dropping propaganda flyers,' said Claude. He handed one to General Fluffington.

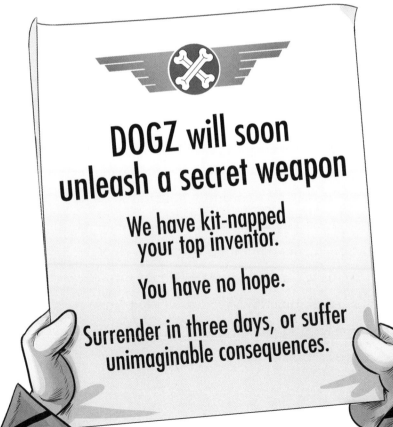

DOGZ will soon unleash a secret weapon

We have kit-napped your top inventor.

You have no hope.

Surrender in three days, or suffer unimaginable consequences.

'This is terrible!' said General Fluffington. 'Cats across Paris will read these DOGZ lies and think they're true!'

'They *are* true,' said Claude. 'It's been several weeks since our chief inventor, C-for, was kit-napped by the DOGZ. They snatched him from right here at CATs HQ! It's like the DOGZ have a spy watching our every move. How are we going to fight this secret DOGZ weapon without C-for's inventions?'

'Ha!' snorted Syd. 'The old geezer's inventions never worked anyway.'

'Correction,' said Claude. 'C-for's inventions never worked as they were *intended*, but they certainly worked. I owe my life several times over to our chief inventor. Without C-for on our side, it won't be long before the whole world's gone to the DOGZ.'

Syd frowned. 'But the DOGZ could have C-for imprisoned anywhere. If only we had a clue.'

'Actually . . .' said General Fluffington. 'We've just received something very interesting. You two had better come and see for yourselves.'

CHAPTER 3

Claude and Syd met up with Commander
Snookums in General Fluffington's office. The
Commander reached into a yellow envelope.

'Just today, we received this photograph of
C-for,' she said, handing the photo to Claude.

'That could be anyone,'
said Claude, squinting closely
and twisting the photo this
way and that, as if it would
make the image clearer.
Commander
Snookums handed
Claude a second photo.

CATs EYES
INTELLIGENCE NETWORK

TOP SECRET FILES

'Crikey dingo,' said Syd. 'That's C-for alright. Only C-for could fall asleep while being kit-napped.'

'One of our contacts, an agent named Smokey, took these photographs,' explained General Fluffington. 'Our CATs Eyes Intelligence Network is spread across the world, wherever Sniffer DOGZ might be poking their noses.'

'Where exactly were these photos taken?' asked Claude.

'Cairo,' said the General. 'We need you in Egypt by tomorrow.'

'Cairo? Egypt? Tomorrow?' said Claude. 'That's over 3000 kilometres away. It's impossible.'

'That's what you think,' said the General.

There was a knock at the door and Mr Tiddles, the General's secretary, popped his head in. Mr Tiddles screwed up his nose and said, 'The head engineer is here to see you sir.'

Claude's friend Manx bowled past Mr Tiddles in her filthy overalls, looking like she'd just emerged from a coal mine.

'Perfect timing,' said General Fluffington. He waved a paw at CATs' head engineer. 'I've asked, um ... what's-her-name here ...' Manx tensed, as the General fumbled for her name. She was terrified of anyone discovering the awful name her parents had given her. 'Ahhh ... thing-a-me-bob ... you know.'

She was saved embarrassment when Commander Snookums cut in. 'Manx. Thank you for joining us,' said the Commander. She turned to Claude and Syd. 'Our head engineer has a new aeroplane for you.'

General Fluffington took over again. 'If these DOGZ really are making C-for work on some secret weapon, there's no time to lose. I want you to follow this up. Make contact with Smokey and bring back our chief inventor. You'll be leaving immediately. Manx, take them down and show them their new kite.'

VICKERS VIMY
LONG-DISTANCE TRANSPORTER/BOMBER

(1) Tail elevators steer the plane up and down

(2) Tail rudders steer the plane left and right

(3) Ailerons help roll the plane to the left and right

(4) Fuselage/hull — constructed of steel tubing covered in fabric

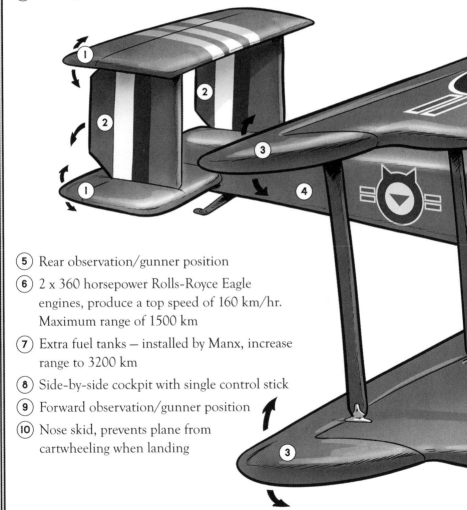

(5) Rear observation/gunner position

(6) 2 x 360 horsepower Rolls-Royce Eagle engines, produce a top speed of 160 km/hr. Maximum range of 1500 km

(7) Extra fuel tanks — installed by Manx, increase range to 3200 km

(8) Side-by-side cockpit with single control stick

(9) Forward observation/gunner position

(10) Nose skid, prevents plane from cartwheeling when landing

Down in CATs' main hangar, Claude and Syd scrambled out of their bandages, while Manx filled the Vimy's petrol tanks.

'As it turns out,' Manx was saying, 'Bomber Command in London have just sent us this brand-new long-distance Vickers Vimy, and they need it tested. I've made a few special modifications – with my extra fuel tanks you'll be able to make the trip in one flight, all 3200 kilometres. It'll be a new world record. Of course you won't be able to tell anyone about it,' she shrugged. 'This is a top-secret mission.'

Just then, Manx's sisters, Picklepurr and Wigglebum, ran into the hangar.

'We've just been at the medical wing,' said Pickle.

'Ith's crazy over there,' Wiggle fizzed.

'I hope you weren't being a nuisance,' fretted Manx.

'I was there to get a medical kit for Claude and Syd's mission,' said Pickle.

'I wath there to get cweam puffs,' added Wiggle, jumping up and down. Manx could see that Wiggle was full of sugar. It was a constant job supervising her sisters as well as CATs' aeroplanes.

Pickle handed Syd the medical kit. 'We've got ointments and bandages for your trip.'

'I just got *out* of bandages!' moaned Syd, throwing up his arms in disgust. 'I never want to be wrapped in bandages ever again!'

'Don't listen to Syd,' said Claude. He placed the medical kit in the main catpit. 'It's very thoughtful of you. I'm sure it will be most useful.'

For a moment Claude worried whether Pickle and Wiggle had told anyone about the secret mission. There was certainly a DOGZ spy at CATs HQ, and Claude didn't know who he could trust.

But soon these worries were cast from his mind as the Vimy sped down the runway. With the extra fuel weight, the Vimy was having trouble getting off the ground. Syd rammed the throttle extra hard and they finally took to the air, barely missing the treetops at the end of the runway. Claude was able to relax once they were airborne and on their way to Cairo. He snuggled up in the forward observation catpit. He'd need all the sleep he could get so he could take over the controls from Syd in seven hours' time.

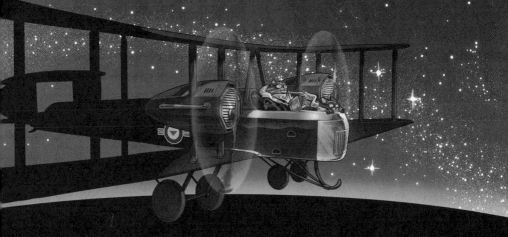

Claude awoke to the drone of engines. He was stiff and sore and bitterly cold. He peeked out of the catpit and was greeted with an icy blast. The sky was the deep blue indigo of night, speckled with a million brilliant stars. Below, the solid black mass of the Mediterranean Sea stretched as far as the curved horizon.

Claude took the controls from Syd, who pointed out their location on the map. Another eight hours to go.

At long last, the horizon grew pale. Claude could see the African coast — a great hazy smudge of purple dunes, waiting for the sun to turn them scorching gold.

As the sky turned pink and yellow, Claude steered the Vimy inland. He shook Syd awake as they headed up the River Nile. The magnificent view opened out, with date palms bending from the river banks like sleepy old men. Soon, Cairo was

passing under their wings in a maze
of alleyways. Blue shadows wriggled
through the ancient city to hidden
places. Dawn's first rays blazed gold
on the spires of the domed mosques,
and the Great Pyramids looked
down over the city just waking up.

CHAPTER 4

Claude and Syd landed just beyond Cairo city, where CATs Bomber Command was setting up an airbase. The ground crew refuelled the Vickers Vimy, but there was no time to rest for Claude and Syd. If that DOGZ pamphlet was true, Claude and Syd had just two days left to rescue C-for. They had to find CATs' secret contact, Smokey, fast. But first they dressed themselves in a disguise so they would blend in with the locals.

The two cats were barely recognisable as they entered the old city. Syd was telling Claude about the times he'd travelled with Claude's dad. 'Your dad always said I looked slimmer in stripes. What do you think?' asked Syd.

Claude shot him a curious glance. 'Do you never stop thinking of your belly?'

'Mate, it's hard to ignore when it's such a big part of me. I just worry that we're *too* well disguised. How will this Smokey recognise us?'

'PSSSST!' A grey cat emerged from the shadows, as if he were stepping out of the ancient stone. The hunched figure hobbled towards them. 'Mr Claude? Mr Syd?' asked the stranger. 'I am your contact, Smokey.'

'How'd you recognise us in our disguise?' said Syd.

'Disguise?' said Smokey. 'I thought you go to fancy-dress party. This modern Egypt, not age of Pharaohs.'

'If Mr Syd want ancient Egypt,'
said Smokey, 'he should visit Professor
Bertie Bell at the Egyptian Museum.'

'Crikey dingo,' Syd exclaimed.
'We don't need to read ancient
hieroglyphs or dig for ruins! Bertie Bell?'
he snorted. 'We don't need some fusty old
geezer who belongs in a museum.'

'You need to blend in better,' said Smokey.
'Dress like an Egyptian. Walk like an Egyptian.'

'Forget that,' said Claude. 'What about C-for?'

'I think, Mr Claude,
you must see for yourself.
Walk this way.'

Smokey hobbled off.
Claude and Syd hunched
over and limped after,
until Smokey turned and said.
'No, I mean, *follow* me.
You can walk normally.'

Smokey took Claude and Syd deep into Cairo's Grand Bazaar, where exotic new wonders lined their way. Stallholders tried to press trinkets into their paws. Colourful silks fluttered from stone archways. They passed teetering towers of silver pots, crouching snake charmers, and sumptuous shops lined with ornate rugs.

Claude's nose twitched at new fragrances — dusty stone and jasmine wafted on the air, while the smell of sugary date cakes and coffee drifted from food stalls and cafés nestled into nooks and crannies.

Different fragrances turned Syd's head. He began drooling as they passed a stall selling hookah pipes and Egyptian catnip.

'No time for that,' said Claude. 'Besides — don't you know that smoking stunts your growth?'

'It hasn't stunted *my* growth,' Syd pouted.

At least not the growth around your middle, thought Claude, dragging his friend away. They were on a top-secret mission, not cruising for catnip.

Smokey led them to a darker part of the bazaar, where cats lay sprawled in open doorways and dogs stared, slack-jawed, from the shadows.

'This is old flea market,' said Smokey. They stopped at a corner, where they had a view of an alley lined with trucks.

'What's so special about these trucks?' said Syd.

Smokey looked nervously around, then snuck along one side of the trucks. He lifted the canvas covers. A DOGZ logo was painted on the side!

'Quick, hide here,' whispered Smokey.

They ducked behind some baskets, where they had a good view.

Several dogs were milling aimlessly, until a small figure appeared and began bossing them around. Claude's eyes bulged when the figure turned their way. The dog had a star over one eye.

'Crikey, isn't that Brutus?' muttered Syd.

It was the DOGZ Spy Master, whom Claude had outsmarted on a previous mission to Venice. 'What's Brutus doing here?' wondered Claude.

'I see this dog with Mr C-for,' said Smokey. 'He put Mr C-for on a truck, at this very spot.'

'Let's take a closer look,' hissed Claude.

'No, no!' cried Smokey, waving his paws frantically. 'Him Star Dog too dangerous. My job done now.' Smokey turned and disappeared into the main bazaar.

Claude and Syd shrugged, and crept closer so they could overhear the dogs.

'Too far to drive,' one of the drivers was saying. 'I think it's too far.'

Brutus turned on the driver with a snarl. 'You don't get paid ta *fink*! Project Sphinx is much too dangerous to be near the city. It needs ta be out in the remote desert.'

Brutus looked around suspiciously before pulling a piece of parchment out of his pocket. 'These are your instructions. Wot-ever you do, don't let these fall into enemy hands. Make sure our precious cargo arrives at the ship on time. When Project Sphinx is launched those CATs will wish they'd never been born. Now get these trucks loaded and gedda move on, before I have you fed to the crocs.'

The driver gave a whistle and there was a commotion as cargo was loaded into the trucks.

'What on earth is Project Sphinx?'
whispered Syd.

'I don't know,' said Claude. 'But if we follow
Brutus, that should lead us to C-for. Hang on . . .
where has the little brute gone?'

Somewhere in the confusion, Brutus had slipped
away. The dogs clanged the tail gates shut, and with a
bang on the side, the trucks began to rumble off.

'We can't let them get away!' exclaimed Claude.
He flung himself onto the last truck,
with Syd leaping close behind.

Claude picked himself up. 'They got away,' he puffed. 'They could be headed anywhere in this endless desert. We'll never find them.'

'We might do,' said Syd. 'I nabbed the instructions Brutus gave the driver.'

'What does it say?'

Syd held up the note.

Claude cocked an eyebrow at his friend. 'It seems we need to pay a visit to some fusty old geezer who can read hieroglyphs.'

CHAPTER 5

'I forgot how much I hate the desert,' grumbled Syd, as he mopped his brow in the shade of a palm tree. They were standing in front of the Egyptian Museum, a solid building of red stone on the banks of the shimmering River Nile. The sun blazed down out of a great blue dome of sky, and the bricks were beginning to bake as the morning turned to noon. The palms rustled in a breeze rising off the river as Claude and Syd headed inside to find Professor Bertie Bell.

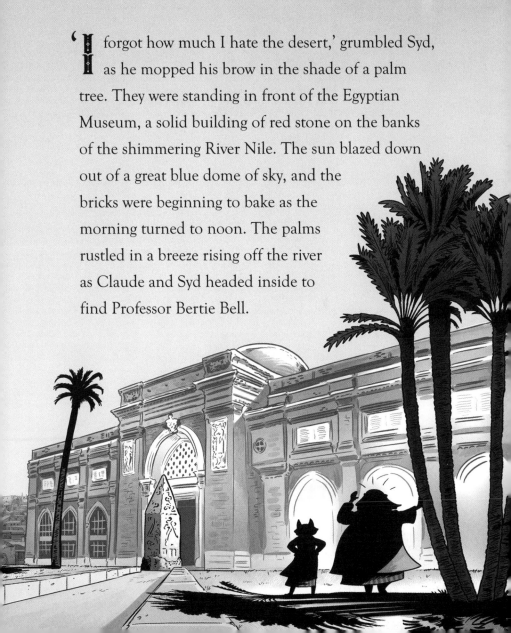

It was pleasantly cool in the museum's vast marble hall. Claude and Syd made their way upstairs, where museum staff were working at desks.

FELINE EVOLUTION

SARCOPHAGUS
EGYPTIAN BURIAL CASKET

'Let's ask that receptionist,' said Syd.

'You fellas look a bit lost,' she said, looking them up and down with a quizzical eye.

'Can we see Professor Bell?' asked Claude.

'Ya sure can.' The cat just stood there.

'Well?' said Syd. 'Where's this Professor Bell?'

'You're lookin' right at her.'

'*You're* Professor Bertie Bell?' snorted Syd.

'You gotta problem with that, mister?'

'Ugggh . . . no . . . it's just that—'

'You thought I'd be some crusty old man?'

Syd looked embarrassed, until the Professor held out her paw.

'Don't sweat it, big fella.' She shook Syd's paw. 'Folks round here call me Bertie, but you can call me Liberty. Liberty Bell. This place is a long way from my home in the U S of A. You two look a long way from home as well.'

'So you didn't mistake us for locals?' asked Syd, slightly disappointed.

Liberty just smiled. 'So whaddaya need a professor of Egyptology for?'

Claude pulled out the parchment with the DOGZ hieroglyphic message. Liberty took one look and

laughed. 'You boys've been flim-flammed. You'll wanna get your money back from the con-man at the bazaar.' Claude and Syd looked dumbfounded. 'This ain't no ancient parchment.'

Now it was Claude's turn to laugh. 'Oh, we're not archaeologists,' he said.

'Of course you ain't, jingle-brains,' said Liberty. 'I thought you were off to a fancy costume party.'

Syd looked even more downhearted.

'We're pilots from CATs,' Claude continued. 'This is a DOGZ coded message.'

A dark shadow passed over Liberty's face. 'DOGZ. I hate those mongrels.'

'The DOGZ have got some new scheme to wipe out all of katdom,' said Claude. 'Something called Project Sphinx. This note has directions to their secret desert base.'

'Can you decode the message?' asked Syd.

'Wouldn't be much of a professor if I couldn't, now would I?' said Liberty. 'I've been reading hiero-glyphs since I was a kit. Now, let's have a little looksie.'

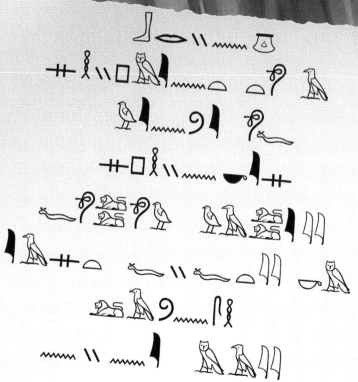

Liberty soon decoded the message, but the meaning was still unclear. 'BRING SHIPMENT TO A VENUE OF SPHINXES?' wondered Liberty.

'Do they mean the Great Sphinx?' asked Claude.

'Too close,' said Liberty. 'The Great Sphinx is just outta Cairo, an' there ain't no valley nearby. Didn't you say these DOGZ have a secret base in a remote part of the desert?' She stroked her chin. 'Ahhh!' she said. 'I got it. It ain't A *Venue* of Sphinxes. It's *Avenue* of Sphinxes.' Syd and Claude looked confused.

Liberty showed them a map. 'The Avenue of Sphinxes is an ancient ruin, in Luxor.'

'This date is tomorrow,' said Claude. 'There's no time to lose.'

'Swell,' said Liberty. 'We oughta get a wriggle on.'

'*We?*' said Syd. 'Impossible! *This* is a CATs top-secret mission and *I'm* senior officer. You're not coming. *Understand?*'

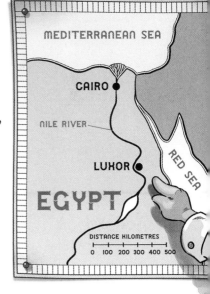

The Vickers Vimy was refuelled and restocked, and the cats were soon on their way.

'You boys need to understand,' Liberty was saying, 'that I'm the type of gal whose courage leaps into action whenever someone says "impossible".'

'Yeah, we noticed that,' grumbled Syd. He was still sour that Liberty had come along.

Claude was at the controls. 'Look on the bright side, Syd. We need someone like Liberty – a cat who knows this desert like the back of their paw.'

'Ya never know what kinda trouble this place'll throw up,' agreed Liberty.

'I don't see any trouble,'
muttered Syd. 'This place is
just one giant sandbox, and
any old cat can dig in the sand.'

Liberty just raised her eyebrows.

The River Nile flowed in a great green path,
snaking through the desert and leading them south
to Luxor.

They flew all afternoon, until the sun became a
giant orange orb as it dropped to the horizon. Darkness
came quickly, and an instant chill swept over the desert
like a cold sheet being pulled over the world.

They flew on to Luxor
through the star-studded night.
Liberty pointed down.
'The Avenue of Sphinxes. Ain't that a sight?'
Claude banked sharply and followed the
valley away from the river.

'We need to land soon,'
said Liberty.

'Not yet,' said Claude.
'Just a little further and we
should find the DOGZ base.'

Liberty pointed directly ahead. 'Whaddya see?'

'Nothing,' said Claude. 'The stars are gone.
Must be cloud.'

'Ain't cloud,' said Liberty. 'It's a sandstorm,
and it's coming much quicker than you think.'

A huge blackness was rising out of the
desert, swallowing the stars as it raced
towards them.

Liberty began rummaging around in the catpit.

'What are you doing?' said Syd.

'Gettin' ready,' said Liberty. 'When ya spend time in the desert, ya get wise to planning and preparing for the worst.' She pulled out a spade and some bandages.

'What's that for?'

'We might need to dig ourselves out. Wrap these bandages around your face.'

They travelled on until they found a clear spot to land. Claude brought the Vimy down in a small valley just as the air began to hum with stinging particles.

Then the sandstorm hit with full force.

They'd barely brought the Vimy to a standstill before the dunes were fizzing with a flurry of tiny tornadoes. Sand began rising and shooting upwards, choking the air like flour through a sieve. It seemed as if the sky had become the desert too.

They constructed a quick canvas shelter under the wing and huddled there, protected from the worst of the battering sandstorm.

'We owe you our lives, Liberty,' said Claude. 'If we'd been caught flying in this . . .' He gave a little shudder. 'How did you get so clever?'

'I owe a lot to my mother,' grinned Liberty. 'She was a swell woman — smart and hard-working. She worked any job she could find to pay my way through university. Later, I learned all about the desert by living and working here in Egypt. We should be safe so long as the storm passes quickly. Now, *I* wanna

hear more about that DOGZ spy.'

'Brutus?' said Claude. 'The one with a star over his eye?'

'Yep, sounds very much like someone I met once.'

Claude told Liberty what he knew of the DOGZ Spy Master. Throughout the night the canvas flapped and cracked. Sometimes the whole aircraft would shudder as if it was about to take off all by itself.

'*Now* I remember why I hate the desert,' griped Syd. 'Claude's dad and I were caught in a sandstorm crossing the Australian Outback. It lasted for three days, and all we had was a car full of stonefish. Why couldn't it have been lobsters?'

CHAPTER 6

Thankfully the sandstorm did not last for three days. By morning, it had moved on leaving the plane half buried in the dunes.

'Lucky you brought this spade,' said Syd.

'Luck!' snorted Liberty. 'Luck ain't nothing to do with it, big fella. I brought this from experience and planning.' She thrust the spade into Syd's paws. 'But *luckily* I planned for you to do all the digging.'

'Weren't you saying any cat can dig in the sand?' chuckled Claude.

'Maybe . . . but I didn't think it would be *me*!' huffed Syd.

They cleared most of the plane, then all three clambered their way to the top of the dune where they were greeted by a surprising view.

It seemed they had landed exactly where they needed to be. The DOGZ convoy was parked amongst pillars and temples that had stood for thousands of years.

Syd looked down through his binoculars. 'They're coming in and out of that tomb.'

'It looks like an archaeological dig,' said Claude.

'Are they looting treasure?' wondered Syd.

'No,' said Liberty. 'Looks like they're takin' treasure *in*. An whaddabout those metal canisters they're carrying?'

'More to the point,' said Syd, 'how are we going to get in? We need to find out what they're up to in there.'

'I've got an idea,' said Claude, 'but you're not going to like it.' He gave his old friend a mischievous grin. 'How many bandages have we got in the medical kit?'

'Are you sure these bandages don't make me look fat?' said Syd. 'It's these horizontal lines. Everyone knows that vertical stripes make you look slim.'

'We'll have a slim chance of getting in if you don't pipe down,' hissed Claude. 'Quick, this way.'

They scampered down the dune and snuck behind the row of trucks. When the workers headed into the cliff face, Claude and Syd jumped into the back of one of the trucks. Syd lifted the lid off a sarcophagus. Luckily, there was no mummy inside.

'Quick, they're coming back!'

They each slid into a casket and waited in the darkness.

There was a scraping and bumping as Claude's casket was lifted out. Behind him, he heard groaning and huffing from the workers.

'By the god Anubis . . . why is this one so heavy?'
Syd was obviously being carried close behind.

Claude's only light came through a crack in the
lid. He was sweating, like a cat on a hot tin roof,
as he was carried across the scorching sand. Then
suddenly the air became blissfully cool and dark.

With a spine-juddering crash the caskets were
dropped on the stone floor. Claude waited until he
heard the footsteps disappearing, then slid the lid off
his casket. Quietly, Syd did the same.

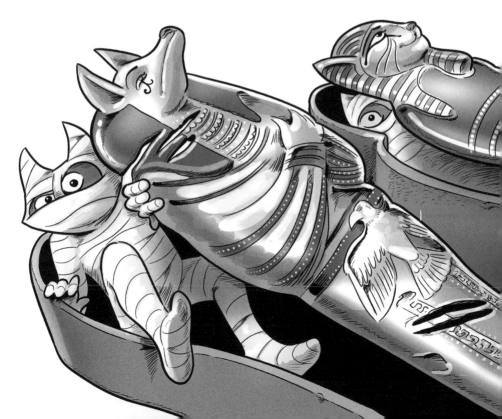

They were deep inside the cliff, in an ancient tomb filled with treasures and metal canisters.

'What in dogs' name are they up to?' whispered Syd. 'If they're not looting the tomb, why are they bringing all this in here?'

Claude nodded in the direction of a side passage. The two cats were about to explore further when a group of guard DOGZ and workers appeared. Syd and Claude stopped dead in their tracks.

Then came the little commander with a star over one eye.

'Commander Brutus,' saluted the guards.

'Wot's this still doin' 'ere?' growled Brutus. 'Start bringing those canisters through. The secret Formula X needs to be added to Project Sphinx. We launch today!'

One of the guards indicated the ancient treasures. Claude held his breath as the guard nudged Syd's bandaged belly. 'What about these mummies?'

Brutus came right up to Claude and pulled at a fraying thread. 'Ship these to The Furrer. Alf Alpha likes ancient treasures, and these mummies are the perfect gift — they come already wrapped!'

Brutus chuckled as he left the guards and workers to shift the artefacts and canisters. When no one was looking, Claude and Syd followed Brutus down a passageway, deeper into the tomb.

There were dozens of side passages, but the two cats followed the click of Brutus's boot heels until they came to a dead end. Brutus was gone!

A sarcophagus stood at the end of the chamber. Claude and Syd raised their eyebrows and Claude touched a finger to his lips.

Slowly, they approached the casket. Syd opened the lid and gave Claude a look.

'What is it?' whispered Claude. But Syd just
squeezed himself inside. There was a lot of grunting
and cursing. The casket was made for a tabby
mummy, not Syd's flabby tummy.

When the lid closed there was a soft whooshing
noise and the grunting stopped.

'Syd?' whispered Claude.

Claude opened the lid . . . Syd was gone! Claude
stepped inside with a worried frown. Was this a
booby trap? Or a secret entrance?

As he pulled the lid shut, there was a soft click
and a scraping of gears on ancient stone.

Suddenly, the space under Claude's feet opened
up. With a whoosh he disappeared down a tunnel.

Claude went tumbling down a curvy slide.
He was just getting under control when he hit the
bottom — in more ways than one . . .

BWOFF!

CRIKEY!

The two cats found themselves in a newly
constructed section of the cave, with steel beams and
modern concrete slabs.

A wide glass window looked out over a cavernous underground chamber. Below, DOGZ in protective suits were coming and going. In the middle of the chamber was a huge apparatus — a cylinder with pipes and fins jutting out of it.

'This must be Project Sphinx,' said Syd.

PSSSSST

Workers came in carrying the canisters from the trucks. Each worker approached the cylinder in the middle of the room.

'What's in those canisters?' wondered Claude.

A worker connected their canister, then pulled a lever. There was a sharp hiss, like some kind of gas was being released into the cylinder.

Suddenly the cylinder began throbbing. It pulsed and rattled. The metal rivets bulged and creaked like something was trying to get out!

A siren split the air.

AWOOOOGAAH!

AWOOOOGAAH!

The workers rushed about, frantically pulling levers and checking dials.

Claude and Syd took advantage of the chaos to shed their bandages and slip into a couple of protective suits.

Claude's voice came out of the suit with a metallic rasp. 'Let's take a closer look.'

They each grabbed a clipboard and made their way down to the workshop floor.

When they got to the bottom, the siren had stopped. Claude and Syd made their way over to the huge cylinder to find out what it was.

'You there!' came a voice.

The two cats froze as a scientist approached.

'How is the payload?'

'Uggh—' mumbled Claude.

Syd flicked through his paperwork, trying to look like he knew what he was doing. Claude tapped a dial.

'Just look through the viewing portal,' said the scientist.

Claude put his eye to a small window. When he saw what was inside, he leaped back with a jerk.

The entire cylinder was jam-packed with fleas. Unnaturally huge fleas! And they looked hopping mad.

An impatient voice cut through the crowd.

'Wot's the status update?' said Brutus.

'It can't take any more,' said one of the scientists. 'Our canisters of Formula X have turned the fleas into crazed, uncontrollable monsters! But luckily no leaks.'

'Lucky for *you*, boffin,' snarled Brutus. 'Or Alf Alpha would hav you thrown to the crocs! We haven't been breeding these super fleas just so we can hav our plans spoiled at the last minute. With this ultimate flea bomb, CATs will be scratched out for good!' Brutus stormed off. 'Proceed with

the launch as planned,' he barked.

So, thought Claude, *Project Sphinx is a gigantic bomb packed with super fleas!* It would cause devastation of the likes never imagined by any civilised creature, and Claude had a pretty good idea of where DOGZ were planning to drop it. Claude and Syd exchanged glances. They had to get out of here and get a message to Bomber Command in Cairo. They had to stop this flea bomb leaving here at any cost.

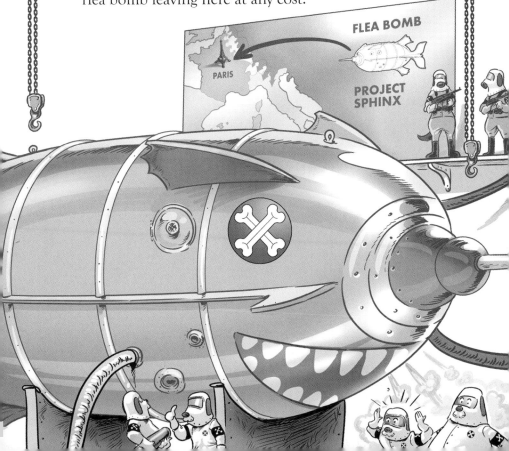

CHAPTER 7

Liberty had finished clearing sand from around the Vimy's wheels. She was quite enjoying herself. As a professor at Cairo Museum, she didn't get out much any more. Digging in the hot Egyptian sun reminded her of her days as a kit, when she'd helped her father dig for dinosaur bones in Montana — *probably causin' more work than helping*, Liberty realised now. She remembered all those snooty cats back in New York, who looked down their noses at her and said, 'Why would you wanna go scratching in the sand? Lil' girls can't be archaeologists. It's simply *impossible*.'

That just made Liberty more determined to prove them wrong. And here she was, all these years later, the head of the Egyptian Museum. She wiped her brow and slumped down under the shade of the wing, covered in sweat and sand. What would those city cats think if they could see her now? A *desert rat?* Liberty laughed to herself.

She took a long gulp of water, then she heard the drone of an engine. It was approaching quickly.

She popped her head into the bright glare of sunlight, shading her eyes — and got a surprising eyeful.

A huge DOGZ airship soared overhead. Liberty clambered up the dunes and looked down, as it flew into the next valley.

The airship manoeuvred slowly until it was hanging above the stony outcrop. Something big was about to happen.

Below, an entire battalion of
DOGZ soldiers had arrived outside
the main entrance to the tomb.

'That don't look good,' Liberty
frowned. Claude and Syd were now
trapped in there.

Liberty gripped her spade.
'There's always a secret entrance
to these ancient tombs,' she said.

Claude and Syd hurried through the vast hangar,
looking for a way out. They hadn't gone far when
DOGZ soldiers began marching in through the
main entrance.

'There goes our escape,' grimaced Claude.

'If we can't get out, at least we can send a
warning,' said Syd. 'Let's find a radio transmitter.'

They passed though an area where DOGZ

scientists and engineers were working away on their evil weapon.

'Sick puppies,' Syd muttered furiously. 'How can they live with themselves, creating Weapons of Mass Distraction?'

Then they saw something that stopped them in their tracks.

There, among the dogs hunched over their workbenches, was an old black cat — and he was wearing a dressing gown!

Claude rushed over with arms spread wide.

'C-for!' he beamed.

The old cat turned, eyeing Claude up and down.
'Yes?'

'It's us!'

'And what do you want now? To take my food
away for not working on your evil bomb? To put me
in kennel confinement for talking to my friends? To
whip me for falling asleep? I'll have you know, sleep
is when I come up with my best ideas!'

'We're here to save you!' said Claude,
exasperated. Then he remembered that he and Syd
were wearing protective suits.

'It's me, Claude.
We're taking you back
to CATs HQ.'

'Come on, you old
geezer,' grumbled Syd.
'Anyone would think
these dogs were your
best mates!'

'They *are* my best mates,' said C-for.

C-for began pointing out his fellow workers. 'There's Jack Russell, all the way from New Zealand; Furnando, from Spain; Jelly, Scotty, Pugsley; and this here is my dear friend Dot.' C-for introduced them to a Dalmatian seated next to him. 'I met Dot long before the war, when we were students in Berlin.'

'C-for wanted to be a violinist,' said Dot. 'And I was going to be a great pianist, playing Woofgang Mozart, Bark and DePussy in all the great concert halls of Europe.' Dot sighed. 'Unfortunately, they said my Bark was worse than my bite.'

'That's nothing,' chortled C-for patting Dot on the back. 'They said *I* sounded like I was strangling a cat! We both ended up studying science instead. And *now* we're both prisoners of the DOGZ army.'

'We've got to get a message out of here,' urged Claude. 'That thing … that monstrous bomb is headed for Paris!'

'Oh, don't fret over that,' said C-for calmly. 'You don't think any *true* scientist would—'

'Would what?' asked Claude, but C-for was fast asleep.

'What C-for was saying,' said Dot. 'Is that the bomb will never reach Paris. You don't need to worry. We built a trigger fault in the design.'

AWOOOOGAH!
AWOOOOGAH!

C-for was woken by the blaring alarm.

'Is that a good siren?' asked Syd.

C-for peered over the tops of his glasses. 'Have you ever known a siren to be good?'

From high above came the giant scraping noise
of stone and gears, and the whine of metal against
metal. The roof of the chamber began to split apart,
and a great gash of blue sky shone down. As the roof
opened wider and wider, an immense DOGZ airship
came in to view.

'Oh dear,' said Dot.

'What do you mean, "oh dear"?' asked Claude.

'The bomb is designed to be carried by that airship,' said C-for. 'And our trigger fault is designed to explode the bomb as soon as it is locked on to the airship.'

'It's gonna explode!' stammered Syd.

Workers began attaching huge chains to the bomb to haul it skyward.

'Quick!' commanded Claude. 'We've got to get out of here!'

'That's another problem,' frowned Dot, rattling her leg. The scientists were chained to their desks.

They were all prisoners!

'There's only one key,' said Jack Russell. 'It has a star-shaped handle.'

'Brutus wears it around his neck,' added Dot.

'Syd will stay with you,' said Claude. 'I'll find Brutus and bring back that key.'

'Thank goodness he has a plan!' said Dot.

'Plan?' said Claude with a mischievous grin. 'I just make it up as I go.' With that, he raced off.

'Hurry Señor Claude,' Furnando called after him. 'El bomba will blow in a matter of minutes.'

Claude's protective suit kept him well disguised from the dozens of guard DOGZ patrolling the facility. He soon discovered Brutus – he wasn't hard to find, because yelling seemed to be the Commander's main job. He barked at someone for looking at him the wrong way, then threatened to throw someone else to the crocs. Then he stomped upstairs to his private office.

Claude followed cautiously, fully aware that time was ticking. He sidled up to the door and removed his helmet. He would need all his senses to strike quickly and silently. *No problem for a cat like me,* Claude thought to himself. He'd been trained in the martial art of Meow-zaki. He slipped inside.

In the darkness he heard Brutus chuckle. 'I should have expected you to turn up … Oh that's right,' smirked the Commander. 'I did.'

The lights flashed on, and Claude was confronted by a squad of guard DOGZ.

'Nab him,' Brutus ordered.

The guard DOGZ charged and Claude leapt into the air with a battle cry …

CHAPTER 8

Liberty ducked and dodged through the darkness. Cobwebs draped across her path and she swiped them out of her way, then brushed her paws on her trouser leg. The ancient Egyptians had built this tunnel as a secret entrance. Liberty had to use all her knowledge and wits, as it was still full of booby traps and wrong turns, designed to foil tomb-raiders. She hoped this tunnel led directly to the original tomb chamber  — that's where the DOGZ would have made their base. Liberty prayed that Claude was hanging around somewhere nearby.

'Claude D'Bonair.' Brutus stretched the words out slowly. 'Fanks for hanging around.'

Despite his martial arts skills, Claude had been overpowered and Brutus had brought him to the original part of the tomb, which had been converted into a research area. A huge domed contraption took up most of the space, surrounded with banks of control panels and pipes jutting out of the time-worn stone.

'You're always turnin' up where you're least wanted,' said Brutus. 'But this time, we were expectin' you. Our little spy at CATs HQ just sent us a major tip-off via our radio transmitter. You won't stop us this time.'

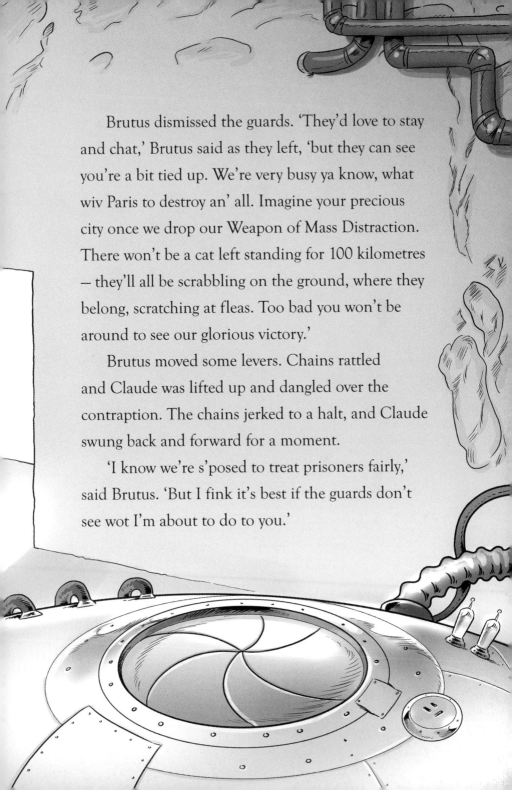

Brutus dismissed the guards. 'They'd love to stay and chat,' Brutus said as they left, 'but they can see you're a bit tied up. We're very busy ya know, what wiv Paris to destroy an' all. Imagine your precious city once we drop our Weapon of Mass Distraction. There won't be a cat left standing for 100 kilometres — they'll all be scrabbling on the ground, where they belong, scratching at fleas. Too bad you won't be around to see our glorious victory.'

Brutus moved some levers. Chains rattled and Claude was lifted up and dangled over the contraption. The chains jerked to a halt, and Claude swung back and forward for a moment.

'I know we're s'posed to treat prisoners fairly,' said Brutus. 'But I fink it's best if the guards don't see wot I'm about to do to you.'

An opening
appeared in the
contraption. Claude
quivered in terror. He
saw the entire insides
were swarming and
moving like a giant black
mass — a vast vat of fleas.

'Welcome to The Flea Pit,' said Brutus. 'It's our
breeding chamber for Project Sphinx. When we add
our Formula X, they become bloodthirsty super fleas.'

Brutus slid one of the levers. There was a
whirring noise and Claude was moved into position
over the opening.

Brutus grinned. 'As you're so insistent on stickin'
your nose into our business, I'd like you to be the first
to get a little taste of our new weapon. Or should I say
— our weapon will have a little taste of you!'

Claude twisted and thrashed his legs as he was
slowly lowered into the pit. There was no escape
this time.

Above the whirring motor Claude heard another sound. A scratching-scrunching sound, almost like a spade hitting rock. He looked up as a section of the wall broke open. With a burst of dust, a scraggly, cobwebbed cat stumbled into the room.

'You!' stammered Brutus.

'You!' spluttered Liberty.

'If you're 'ere for a rescue, you're too late.' Brutus slammed the lever down hard. The chains rattled and Claude began free-falling.

Claude panted as Liberty lowered him to the floor. 'You . . . definitely saved . . . one of my nine lives that time. But . . . how do you know Brutus?'

'From before the war,' said Liberty. 'He swindled the Egyptian Museum out of some precious artefacts — sacred objects, that belong here in Egypt. Brutus was selling them to rich buyers around the world.'

'Seems like Brutus found his perfect master in Alf Alpha,' said Claude.

'Well, the little brute ran into my spade,' said Liberty. 'Is he still alive?'

Claude checked for a pulse. 'There's life in the old dog yet,' he laughed. Claude grabbed the star-shaped key from around Brutus's neck.

They left Brutus unconscious on the floor, then looked out over the base. Pulleys whirred as the bomb was lifted up to the airship.

'Now we have the key to free the scientists,' said Claude. 'But how will we all escape with guard DOGZ blocking every exit? We're running out of time. When that bomb goes off, it's all over.'

'It ain't over till it's over,' said Liberty. 'I got a plan.'

It was an unlikely group that were escaping through the secret tunnels Liberty had discovered – the two CATs pilots, a professor of Egyptology, a crazy inventor and several dog scientists.

'Watchit,' warned Liberty. There were still booby traps, set for ancient grave-robbers.

They came to a passage which led in four different directions.

'What do these hieroglyphs say?' asked Syd.

'One means sunlight and another represents certain doom,' said Liberty.

'Okay, let's follow the light.'

'Not so quick,' said Liberty, holding out an arm. 'The scarab beetle holding the sun can also mean rebirth — in which case, it would lead us right back into the heart of the tomb.'

'Awwwwww!' wailed Syd. His yowl echoed about the chamber. Instead of fading away, it grew into growls and yaps coming from behind them. Guard DOGZ had sniffed out their escape!

'What about these other two doors?' urged Claude. 'What do those symbols mean?'

'Well, one door is to the men's bathroom and the other is for women,' said Liberty.

Another howl echoed after them — the DOGZ were closing in.

'I think I came this way,' said Liberty quickly leading them into the passage with Sobek, the crocodile-headed god of certain doom.

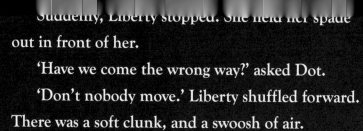

Suddenly, Liberty stopped. She held her spade
out in front of her.

'Have we come the wrong way?' asked Dot.

'Don't nobody move.' Liberty shuffled forward.
There was a soft clunk, and a swoosh of air.

PING CLANG DING

Poisonous darts shot out of nowhere. They bounced harmlessly off Liberty's spade. 'This is the way alright,' she grinned. 'I hadda deal with that lil' trap on my way in. It should take care of our pursuers if they come this way.'

Syd nudged Claude. 'Geez mate. I knew it was a good idea to bring someone with a spade who can read hieroglyphs.' Claude just rolled his eyes.

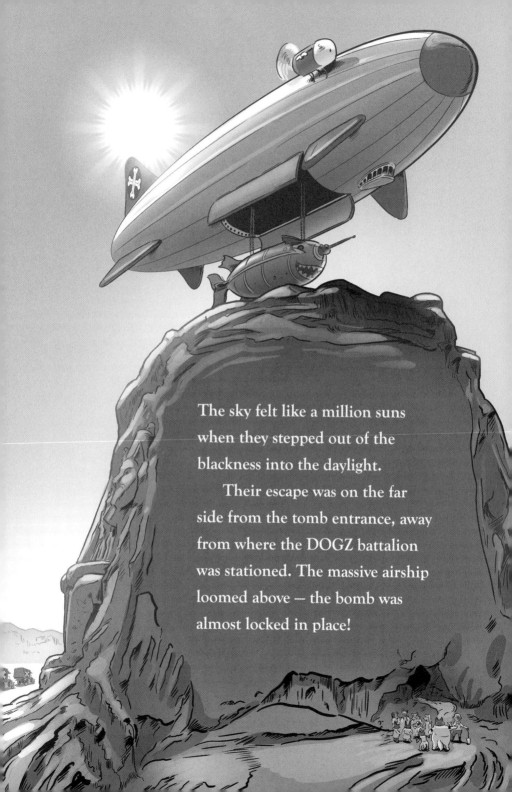

The sky felt like a million suns when they stepped out of the blackness into the daylight.

Their escape was on the far side from the tomb entrance, away from where the DOGZ battalion was stationed. The massive airship loomed above — the bomb was almost locked in place!

Claude was amazed at the bravery of the scientists. They had been prepared to sacrifice themselves to save Paris. Liberty had led their escape, but they weren't safe yet.

'That bomb will destroy everything for miles,' said C-for.

Dot patted her old friend on the back. 'You cats need to take off. We dogs will borrow one of those trucks.' Dot turned to Liberty. 'Thank you for giving us our freedom – our liberty – back.'

'Forgedda-bout-it,' grinned Liberty. 'Liberty's my middle name. No, seriously. My real name is Lamington Liberty Bell.'

C-for hugged his old friends, hoping they would see each other again in better times.

The cats scaled the dune and ploughed down the tumbling sand into the next valley. They flung on their flight suits and leapt aboard the Vickers Vimy.

Claude started the two Rolls-Royce Eagle engines, which burst into life with a bang and a cloud of smoke.

At that same moment another thing burst with a tremendous bang.

The four cats glanced back at the stony outcrop. A second later, a tremendous shockwave rocked the air. The airship was collapsing! A vast cloud of blackness was billowing and engulfing the mountain. It hit the base and began spreading outwards at a terrific speed.

'This is gonna be close,' said Syd, as Claude
thrust the throttle forward. The flea cloud burst
over the top of the dunes, swarming into the valley,
as dangerous and deadly as a living sandstorm. The
Vimy dashed and bounced over the hot sand, with
flea-filled fingers of blackness clutching at the tail.

'We're too heavy,' yelled Liberty, casting off
excess equipment. With a last thrust of power, the
Vimy took to the air.

Below them, the flea-bomb cloud rolled out in
all directions. Claude spotted Dot and the other

scientists safely speeding away.

Claude, Syd, Liberty and C-for cheered for joy, at the thrill of their escape. Behind them settled the dust of disastrous devastation.

'Those fleas won't last long out here in the desert sun,' said Liberty.

Claude shuddered to think of the unimaginable horror such a weapon would have wreaked on his beloved Paris. But thanks to Liberty, they had saved katdom *and* destroyed Project Sphinx.

'Being kit-napped is *not* all it's cracked up to be,' grumbled C-for. 'Was about time you rescued me. Tonight's supper was dog roll again. First thing back in Paris I'm going to—'

'You'll what?' asked Claude. But C-for was having a kit nap of a different kind.

Claude smiled, and headed the Vimy on to Cairo. It would be a sad  farewell when they dropped Liberty back at the Egyptian Museum, but there'd be a big welcome party waiting to greet them when they brought CATs' chief inventor safely home to Paris.

It was several days before Brutus dragged his sorry, flea-bitten hide all the way to The Hound's Tooth, Alf Alpha's mountaintop lair, in the heart of DOGZ territory.

Some might say that The Furrer was *already* crazy, but he went *even* crazier when he heard that Project Sphinx had been foiled by a certain pilot from CATs HQ. He sulked in bed for over a week and refused to talk to Commander Brutus.

Eventually Alf Alpha called in his top commander, General Dogsbody.

'Et tu, Brutus,'* he said, inviting his disgraced commander in as well. Brutus entered timidly, now looking like a small lapdog – a trembling, broken shadow of his former self. 'There, there,' said Alf Alpha, patting Brutus on the head. 'We all have setbacks, and I am not one to complain or whine and make petty plans for revenge.'

PAT
PAT
PAT

* 'And you Brutus'. Famously spoken by Roman Ruler Julius Caesar.

Brutus gave a sigh of relief. 'Some say you're *small*-minded, My Furrer, but thank you for giving me a second chance. Next time we won't have any *little* problems.'

The Furrer's eyes began twitching strangely, and his face turned a dangerous beetroot colour. His ears lay back and his teeth showed in an unnatural smile. '*Small*-minded?' hissed Alf Alpha. '*Next* time? *Little?*' Alf Alpha burst out of bed. 'There will be no *next* time! There will be no *little* problems, and NOTHING about me is SMALL!' screamed Alf Alpha. 'I never want to see you again! GET HIM OUT OF MY SIGHT!'

As Brutus was escorted from the room, the DOGZ leader calmed himself down before continuing. 'So our little desert project did not pan out. I am not concerned with Weapons of Mass Distraction any more. We have a new plan.'

He turned to the fluffy bear in bed next to him.
'Don't we, Edward? Yes we do, yes we do!'

General Dogsbody shuffled nervously at this new strategy. 'DO YOU HAVE A PROBLEM?' screeched Alf Alpha.

General Dogsbody shook his head vigorously.

'Good,' said Alf Alpha, sliding back into his bed. He gave an evil smirk. 'Our spy at CATs HQ is ready to strike. As for this Claude D'Bonair … he has meddled in our affairs one too many times. As soon as The Red Setter is recovered, he will make a dog's dinner of Claude once and for all. *Bwha ha ha ha ha*!'

When Donovan Bixley was young he used
to draw and then write stories to go with his
pictures. When he grew up, he learned that you
were supposed to write the words first. But to tell
you a secret ... Donovan still makes books as he
did when he was a boy.

Two of his books have been named in the
International Youth Library's list of the top 200
children's books in the world, and he is the
recipient of the Mallinson Rendel Illustrators
Award from the NZ Arts Foundation.

Find out more about Donovan and his work
at www.donovanbixley.com